About the author: Mary is a beloved
mother, grandmother, great grandmother,
retired registered nurse, and a published author.

About the illustrator: Geraldine Buteyn is
a wife, mother, grandmother, artist,
retired art teacher, and published illustrator.

The Little Snowflake

By Mary A Rens

Illustrated by Geraldine Buteyn

Once upon a time when it was
quite cold outside the
Little Snowflake was way . . . .

. . way

. . . way

. . . way

up in the sky.

One day in the wintertime it was time for the Little Snowflake to float gently down to the earth.

Down, down, down it floated.

The Little Snowflake noticed that it was not alone. There were lots of other snowflakes floating down.

Each one was a little different, but all of them were so beautiful.

Soon they were all on the ground. Oh, how beautiful they made everything look!

The trees, grass, fields, houses and streets were all covered with snow.

It wasn't long before the Little Snowflake heard some children playing. The children were having such a good time.

Suddenly he felt himself rolling over and over with his snowflake
friends packed all around him.

Soon the children finished making them into
a large snowman. The children added a carrot
for a nose, pieces of coal for the eyes and
buttons, sticks for arms, and a scarf around
it's neck.
How happy the Little Snowflake was to see
the children enjoying the snowman that they
had made.

Each day as the children went by on their way to school they would wave
and say, "Hi, Mr Snowman!"

There were many more days
of winter and the snowman
continued to stand tall.

Days went by. The winter was over and spring came.
The weather became warmer and warmer and the snowman started to melt. The Little Snowflake felt himself turning into water.

Down the street the Little Snowflake flowed. It went this way and that way, and that way and this way, until finally the Little Snowflake flowed right into a big lake.

The Little Snowflake was so happy again because he saw the children.

They were having so much fun swimming with him in the lake!

Then on a very hot and sunny day, the Little Snowflake felt as if he was being lifted out of the water.

Up, up, up he went.

Finally he reached a white fluffy cloud way up in the sky.

And there he waited....
until on a cold winter day he could float down to the earth
once more

as a beautiful Snowflake.

To our great grandchildren

Collin Doerr
Maeva Haveman
Natalie Paul
Evalyn Paul
Brayden Doerr
Ainsley Haveman
Kolden Doerr
Ian Blank
Charlottee Paul
Camden Rens
Ingrid Blank
Rylee Rens
Josalyn Marshall
Reece Rens
Ava Rens

Made in the USA
Middletown, DE
14 January 2019